Naughty Boys Get Spanked

A collection of short stories of humiliation, BDSM, and the erotic touch only a Femdom can provide

Claire Elliott

Table of Contents

Total Obedience

After a long working week in the hospital, it was finally Friday night. I was lucky to get the night off. Usually, I would be working the night shift, trying to get some extra money for the car I want to buy. But not tonight. Tonight, I was going out with some of my friends to a new bar called The Terrace.

I had known these guys for a long time, we had done our training together, and I knew that even though we hadn't seen each other for a while, it was going to be a fantastic evening.

I arrived at The Terrace first and ordered a drink. It wasn't long before the other guys were there and we all decided to try out the specialty beers, and some tapas. Around 11 o'clock, one of us suggested going to a different bar, which was on the same square as The Terrace. The bar he suggested was not as nice as The Terrace, and we knew it's reputation for being the kind of place people go to hook up, but at that point, we were all ready to find a beautiful woman to try and seduce. I downed my beer just as the music became a bit loud and followed my friends out onto the street.

We walked down the road, laughing and making jokes, and it didn't take long before we were at the bar ordering more drinks. After looking around for a while and making some pointless jokes, I saw a woman standing in the middle of the dance floor. She was with a girlfriend, and it looked like they were having fun together. She was wearing a lovely jumpsuit, and it was clear that she could dance well. We were getting closer and closer as we both danced, and I thought for a moment that she was looking at me. Or was that just my imagination, my hope that she looked at me because I had been staring at her for quite some time? She did something to me, and I wanted to know more about her. I gathered all my courage and decided to ask what her name was. To my surprise, she replied, saying her name was Rachel, and we started talking, and she even laughed at some of my jokes.

Unfortunately, the venue was not overly exciting for Rachel and her friend, and they left without giving me her number. When I had asked for it, she just laughed at me and said that if I wanted to have her number, I'd have to do better than that. I only had the first name, and I had to deal with it.

That night in bed, I couldn't get her out of my head. I was staring at the ceiling and could count all the individual strokes of paint. I felt as though I was going crazy thinking about her and decided that I needed to know who she was. After a long search through various online links, I finally found her profile. For the second time that evening, I gathered up all my courage and sent her a request before going to bed and dreaming about her. The way her hair had tumbled down her back in long blonde waves, the crimson color of her lipstick, the way her hips swung in time to the music.

The birds woke me up early the next morning, and for a moment, I was annoyed until I remembered what I had done the night before. Jumping up out of bed, I ran to my computer and logged on to see that she had accepted my request. My stomach was tight with butterflies, and I fist-pumped the air in excitement before I sent her a message. She was online, and to my surprise again, and we started talking. It quickly went from everyday things like bucket list topics to something far darker. I was a little embarrassed to tell her that I wanted to be dominated when she asked me what my greatest fantasy was. I told her that I had tried a bit of BDSM here and there with tying and blindfolds and other 50-shades imitations, but I still missed something. She took a long time to reply, and I thought that I had blown it as the time ticked by, 5 minutes, and then 10 minutes. As time ticked by 15minutes, I finally got a reply. She told me she to had the same problem of finding sexual partners that couldn't give her what she was truly after. I was shocked that she was so forthcoming about what type of kink she was interested in and almost had a heart attack when she told me that she had been a Mistress for several years. We talked for another hour before she had to go and get ready for work, as she worked as a Police Officer and worked on a different roster than the typical 9-5. I understood that with the whole nursing thing.

For months we messaged. Sometimes she would call me, but she made it clear that I was not to call her. I obeyed, not wanting to annoy her or for her to lose interest in me. I had had a Mistress in the past, but Rachel was different. She didn't make me feel like we had a dynamic straight off the bat as that other woman had; she took her time to get to know me first. She would ask me things like what I wanted to do with my life, what kind of problems did I find with myself, and what parts of myself I loved. She asked if I would like to enter into a virtual agreement where I wasn't to have sex with anyone for a month and that I had to do some small tasks for her. To my disappointment, she didn't want me to call her Mistress and told me to strictly call her Rachel as we got to know each other.

Two months passed, and I thought my hand would break with all the wanking I was doing. Rachel made me take videos every time I jerked off, and she had laughed when one day, I sent her 13 of them. After that, she put a limit on how many times I could wank, it was three times a day, and I wasn't sure how I was going to manage that. I know that I could have done it without her knowing, but I loved that denying myself came from wanting to please her. As the three-month mark approached, Rachel did something completely unexpected. She suggested meeting again and seeing what would happen. I felt a leap inside my stomach and a tingling sensation in my cock that had become uncomfortably hard and pinched in my pants. I was grateful that I still had one jerk time left for the day and decided to relieve myself in the shower.

Over the next few days, we arranged a time, and she instructed me on what she wanted me to bring. She told me to bring a towel, clamps, the lube I like to use and rope. We discussed what a scene would look like, what kind of aftercare I like, and she told me her expectations for the night. It was everything I had dreamed of, a woman women wanting to dominate me after I proved to her that I was worth her time, perfect.

On a warm late summer afternoon, I arrived at the address she gave to me. It was the house of her friends where she was staying. Her friends were on vacation, so she was looking after their home. I messaged her that I was out the front like she had instructed to do, and she opened the garden door. She was incredibly beautiful in the light of the club where we had seen each other before, but the light of the sun made her even more attractive. I was taken aback by her smile. She didn't seem to be the hard Mistress she had told me she was. She was wearing a tight black shirt with flowy pants. I secretly looked at the contours of her breasts and her ass and felt my cock tingle and feel warm inside. I smiled to myself as she led me up the path and toward that house. I couldn't help but think how beautiful she was.

She led me into the living room, and I saw that she had already set up coffee and tea with a selection of small cakes elegantly placed on fine china. She tilted her head to suggest I should sit down, and following her instruction. I sat obediently.

We talked about how our week had been, what kind of work issues had arisen, and she asked about the car I was still saving for. I liked that she seemed interested in my life and didn't make me feel like just another hookup. As we sat and talked, ate, and drank into the late afternoon, the sunset behind the hills in the distance, and she asked me if I wanted something else to drink.

She went to the kitchen. I followed her and said that I didn't need anything, but asked if she wanted anything that I could get her. Suddenly she turned around and stood close to me. She asked me if I felt comfortable; she said she knew that I had been quite tense from the moment she opened the garden door. I answered yes before she suddenly grabbed my neck and kissed me passionately on my mouth. I responded to her kiss, and everything began to play in my mind. I could never have expected that I could kiss this woman. She looked at me with her beautiful eyes and grabbed me with a hand around my mouth.

"So, you wanted to be an obedient slave?" She asked in a stern voice. I nodded yes, and she laughed.

"Do you think you can please me?" Again I nodded yes without saying anything. She slapped my cheek and asked if I had lost my tongue.

"Yes," I answered — another blow, this time harder.

"I will explain this to you one time tonight, slave. From now on, I am Mrs. Shelby or Mistress to you. If I ask you for something, your answer will always end with Mistress, do you understand?" A harder blow followed.

"Yes, Mistress, I understood." She forced me to take off my clothes and stood in front of me. She looked at my hard cock disapprovingly and laughed.

"Is that all you got slut? Do you think you're doing me a favor with this? I can use my fingers even better than anything you will be able to do. I'm going to get ready. Kneel on your knees and wait until I get back." She commanded, watching as I followed her instructions before disappearing into another room. I heard her opening and shutting cupboard doors and the unmistakable sound of a zipper.

I had been kneeling on the hard kitchen floor for ten minutes before I saw her come back. I could feel the beginnings of my knees hurting, and I liked that she patted my head as she passed me and went to get a glass of water. She had put on a beautiful latex jumpsuit, and her hair sat back in a ponytail. I felt my cock harden again and saw precum run out of me and drip onto the floor. My Mistress saw this, too, and a hard blow followed. She secured a collar around my neck with a belt attached to it. Using the belt, she pulled my head to the kitchen floor.

"You are going to lick this up slut; everything must be spotless. When I'm done with you, you will learn how delicious it is to get your cum in your mouth!" I licked the floor, thanking a higher force that it was clean, apart from the mess I had made. When she was satisfied, she forced me to get up. She was surprisingly strong as she held me up as the blood ran back into my legs, making me wince in pain. She liked that, and I think that she only kept holding me so she could watch how painful it was as pins and needles began to pierce my calves. When I was able to stand on my own, she led me to the couch. She lay down on her back and spread her legs. The latex jumpsuit, with a double zipper. She looked at me and asked, "Do you think you are worth it slut?"

"Yes, Mistress, I think I am worth it." She unzipped the bottom of the jumpsuit and slowly pulled it aside. Roughly, my mistress pulled on the belt and buried my face in her pussy. I felt her warm moisture run down my nose and lips and tasted the delicious sweetness.

"Lick slut, see if you can deliver something delicious to your mistress." I licked her lips and kissed them, after which I slowly went to the burdock. I saw her pelvic floor collapse and got excited that she liked it. I was doing something right. The contraction became more and more rhythmic, and I heard a loud moan, "Well done, slut, you can go on." My face was pushed into her pussy again, and she came again. She moaned with pleasure, and I felt more cream coming out of my cock. I grabbed it with my hand before it fell to the floor. My mistress grabbed my hand and forced me to wet her ass hole.

"Put two fingers in me now!" I obeyed. This was new to me, and I should never have done this. I felt the rhythmic contraction even more and got the feeling that another orgasm was coming. Again my Mistress came, and this time, a small stream of fluid came out that came directly into my mouth. I tasted the sweetness and almost had to make an effort not to cum myself.

My Mistress took my collar and pushed me away.

"Well done, slut, you've done your best. If you obey, you may someday replace your fingers with that little dick of yours. I can't wait to get fucked in my ass while weights are hanging on your balls that are tickling against my clit and pussy ". She forced me back onto the hard kitchen floor and held my face. I wanted to sit down but felt something against my butt hole.

"Mistress, there's something in the way," I said anxiously. "No slave, that is especially for you." I looked behind me to see a lube covered butt plug suctioned to the floor. The red butt plug, specially selected at its 6 cm thickness, was now ready to take me. I wanted to sit carefully, but suddenly, Mistress sat down on my lap. I could not stop it and sank to the kitchen floor and felt my butt spread as the thick butt plug filled me. I moaned in pain and pleasure. A hard blow followed.

"Did I say you could make a sound slut?" My Mistress said as she slapped my face.

"No, Mistress," I replied as she slapped the other cheek.

"I thought so," said Mistress, "I have a solution for that. God, I am smart." With that, I got a ball gag pushed into my mouth that was tightened hard.

"Well, that's better, hey slut? Now I don't want to hear from you anymore!" My Mistress stood up and watched as I sat on the plug. She smiled as she began to rub her breasts. I was happy that my pain was bringing her pleasure, and I was rewarded by her standing close to me and letting me rest my head on her thigh as she stroked my hair for several minutes.

When I relaxed and pressed my head into her, she smiled and looked down at me. She smiled lovingly before switching back to the strict Mistress, who had forced the plug into my ass. She stepped back, and before I could register what was happening, she had tied me to the floor. My Mistress knelt by my head and whispered, "You are my slut now; you can't go anywhere. I'm going to do everything I want with you, and it's all for my pleasure!" I nodded yes before I was blindfolded and suddenly felt my Mistress running her fingernails over my nipples. Pinching them until I gasped around the ballgag in my mouth as her fingernails were replaced with sharp pains on both my nipples.

Clamps, I thought, and I felt the serrated edges in my nipples. My body came alive with pain as she secured what felt like clothes pegs to my torso. I felt something cold with my cock and heard the click of a lock. Then I felt a stabbing pain in my cock and realized that my Mistress had found the chastity cage that I had secretly brought with me. My blindfold went off, and I could see what had been done to me. My Mistress raised an eyebrow at me before flicking the chastity cage with her foot making me groan. The chastity cage was wrapped around my cock, with a tube slid into my cock that would control and prevent my flow of cum. There were clamps on my nipples. Does she not want to see my cock anymore because it is not worthy? I felt my cock harden and intense pain shoot through my body. I tightened everything and felt the thick butt plug against my prostate. These feelings only made me even more excited, and I suddenly felt all the tension drifting away. I wanted to give my Mistress everything. I wanted to give her delicious orgasms, total surrender, total obedience, whatever she wanted as I felt my mind drift into the place that felt like I had come alive from the most relaxing sleep, as though I was breathing for the first time.

I was roughly ripped out of my thoughts by loud

blows of a whip on my body. My Mistress waiting until my eyes focused on her. She held my gaze, and I knew what she wanted from the planning that we had done before today. She wanted me to look at her while she whipped me, wanting me to know that it was her who had given me this feeling. Nothing was spared, my cock, my nipples, my thighs with every blow, my cock became harder and the pain more intense. My Mistress smirked before she whispered in my ear, "I think the pegs look good, but I want the result. Do you know what I'm going to do right now, little slut? "I excitedly hoped that she would open the pegs and remove them. Another blow and 1 of the pegs flew off my body with the intense pain of letting go and the slap of the Mistress.

"Count them," Mistress commanded. I muffled the count around my gag, forgetting where I was up to causing another crack of her whip across my ass. After I reached number 20, I lay still and moaned. My mistress seemed satisfied. She grabbed my cock and pulled the tube out of my cock. A whole stream of seed came and landed on her hand.

"So slut, you've saved up! Now it's time to give it back to you," and she pushed the fingers with my puddle of cum along with the ball gag into my mouth. I tasted my cum, and it made me even hotter. The total surrender and humiliation made me more and more excited and even drove the continuous pain in my cock through the chastity cage.

My mistress noticed this, and I got blindfolded again. The ball gag went out of my mouth, and I felt her mouth whisper in my ear.

"So slut," she said in a soft voice. It gave me a wonderful shiver and a warm feeling.

"So, do you like your cum deep in your throat?" Before I could answer, she opened my mouth and pressed something deep down my throat. It felt soft and smooth, and at first, I thought it was her latex, elbow-long gloves.

"Lick slut," I heard my Mistress say. I

started to lick the object and soon realized that it was in the shape of a cock. My Mistress grabbed my head and started making jerking movements with her hips. I realized that she had put on a strap-on and that she was now fucking my mouth. The dildo could not have been a millimeter thicker as I opened my mouth as wide as I could to take it.

"You have a big mouth, slut. This dildo is 6cm thick, and it just fits in your mouth. You like it, huh? You like it when I waste my time humiliating you, don't you?" I nodded yes, which again gave me a series of punches with the dildo in my mouth. My Mistress pulled out the dildo as a stream of saliva poured from my lips and over my face.

"Well done, slave, you learn quickly, but I think you can do even better. You're such a good boy. You can be better for me, can't you?" Again the dildo disappeared into my mouth, and I was fucked again in my mouth by my Mistress. She grabbed handfuls of my hair as she rammed my mouth, making me gag on her cock as she owned me.

Suddenly she stopped, and I felt how she took the cage off my cock. I sighed in relief as she did, making her laugh and kiss my cheek, making me blush. She took off my blindfold and pushed the strap-on to one side as she bent over.

"So pretty slut, now you can prove how well you can fuck. If I am not satisfied, then punishment and torture will follow!" She said while looking me in my devoted eyes. I knew they had the glaze of surrender in them, and I'm glad she noticed to by the affectionate pat she gave my face before standing back up. It didn't take long to make my cock hard, and she lay down as I climbed on top of her. I knew not to keep her waiting and thrust into her with as much power as I could muster. She gave a short moan, but I soon saw that this did not have the effect I had hoped. She started to laugh and pushed me away from her. I hated myself for not being able to please her and blushed before looking down in humiliation.

"Do you call that fucking slut? I don't even

feel anything happening. You have fucked a woman before, haven't you? Have you lost your dick? Can't get him to do what you want him to? I think it's time for some re-education baby slut." She took the collar and fastened it around my neck tightly before she took me to another room. Here was a small bench with various fastening buckles. She laid me down on the bench and tied my hands and ankles. My neck was also tied to the bench.

"So slut, I'll show you how to fuck someone." I felt the lubricant on my ass, followed by the biggest dildo I had ever had in my ass. I moaned with pleasure and heard my Mistress do the same. I turned around and saw that she was kneading her breasts while she mercilessly hit my ass. I felt how the dildo filled me up and saw more juices coming out of my cock with each thrust. My Mistress caught it and smeared it on my face and put it in my mouth, followed by a few blows. I felt the punches getting faster, and I knew my Mistress was going to cum. I had a wonderful feeling inside. I could please my Mistress and even let her cum by taking me. My Mistress continued to fuck my ass, spanking me until I could feel my ass cheeks going red before she suddenly came shockingly while she hit the dildo extra deep in my ass.

"You let yourself be taken by large objects slut. If you can handle the next test, then I have a reward for you, something special from me ". I felt my ass spread with the left hand of my Mistress and then felt my ass stretched to the maximum. I felt an object with some protruding points slowly sliding into my ass. I wanted to look back, but as I turned my head, my Mistress slapped my face.

"Are you ready for this slut?" I answered by simply nodding my head and felt my ass stretch even further and suddenly relaxed. Had my Mistress inserted the butt plug? Then I felt something rhythmically go back and forth in my ass, something that was much bigger than the butt plug. I felt the object move, and with a shock, I realized that my Mistress had put her whole hand in me. My fantasy became a reality down to the last detail. I felt how my Mistress put her second hand inside me, and I could hardly hold it when this, too, started to move rhythmically with the other. I moaned with pleasure until I almost finished. At that moment, my Mistress stopped, and I got a few hard slaps on my ass.

"You haven't earned an orgasm slut yet, and maybe you won't get it tonight." She released me and forced me to lie on my back. I felt the wetness of my seed on the bench, mixed with the lubricant that ran out of my ass when my Mistress worked on me with her fists. I was out near exhaustion, more psychologically than physically.

My mistress came to sit with her pussy on my chest so that I could look at her from below.

"I promised you something very special, entirely from myself, because you spoiled me so well. If you accept this gift, then your surrender to me is complete, and you are my slut."

"I do everything for you, mistress, and I would like to accept your special gift." My Mistress moved forward so that her pussy was pressed directly into my face.

"Open your mouth. Stick out your tongue slut, now!" I opened my mouth and watched as she began to play with herself on top of me. She rubbed her finger over her clit before diving her fingers into her pussy and edging herself near to orgasm. She continued to tease herself before suddenly, I felt her warm liquid squirt on my tongue as she came hard. My mistress stroked my head with her hands and pushed my face deeper into her pussy.

"Drink from me, dirty slut, proof that you have everything for me!" She pinched my nose and forced me to drink her cum. When she was done, she slapped my face dismissingly.

"Well done slut, you proved that you do everything for me. Because you have behaved so well, the next session will be even more special. My other slave has behaved even better than you, and I have allowed him to have a one-time chance to show how his dominant side is. Of course, I will assist him in every step of the process. I am glad that I finally have a suitable test object that is as willing as you are." She pulled on my collar and led me to the basement, where there was a mattress with a blanket.

"Think carefully about what happened to you and prepare yourself for what is coming. I will be back in a little while to make sure you are alright and to give you some special attention for being so wonderful tonight." After she spoke these words, the door closed and locked, and I was left alone in the dark. My imagination was fulfilled, and a sense of great satisfaction passed through me as I tasted my mistress and felt the last bit of sperm run out of my cock and lube from my ass. Then I fell asleep satisfied.

Horny Mistress

It had been two weeks since I had answered the online add on the Mistress and Naughty Boy site. I had been a member of the site for a little over a month before I saw that add and was excited that the Mistress in question had seemed pleased with me, so much that she requested to meet me in person. She had given me strict instructions on what to wear and how to prepare myself, and having obeyed her to my highest ability, I stood outside the iron gates of her lavish country home.

She had told me she only received only nice boys in school uniform. Although it had been several years since I had worn such a thing, the uniform which she prescribed was familiar to my own schooling days. The uniform had to consist of a white, fitted and fully buttoned shirt, a perfectly buttoned and tightly tied school tie, and a fitted sweater with V-neck vest, a uniformed blazer, white underpants, short blue uniform pants, socks, and shoes — nothing more, nothing less. Finally, I also had to cut my hair into a modern style and have it washed fresh neatly.

So I presented myself at the agreed address, a chic country house on the outskirts of the city. A girl who introduced herself as a chambermaid opened the door. She led me to a waiting room, explaining that Mrs would receive me momentarily. In the meantime, I would get some reading material. The girl left me alone in the waiting room, where I stood up a little indecisively. Then I heard someone approaching, and a good-looking lady appeared in the doorway, whom I recognized immediately. She was even more beautiful in person, and although we had not discussed her age, I estimated that she would be in her late thirties. She wore expensive and sexy looking clothes, a white blouse with a black tie, and black leather pants. She was wearing black leather boots with stiletto heels.

"Look at it, what a neat schoolboy," she said mockingly, "that's how I like it," and kissed me on the lips. I blushed and did not mumble anything other than, "of course, Mrs."

"So you will get your instructions from me," she explained, "and I demand obedience and nothing less. Discipline and rules are important in this house, and violations are punished according to the house rules." I didn't look at her understandingly.

"Didn't Tammy give you any house rules yet?" Mrs asked, frowning slightly. I shook my head, remembering that she had told me she didn't like non-verbal behavior very much. I quickly replied, "No, Mrs, but I will obey your instructions." She smiled.

"You are also to uphold your end of this deal because otherwise, you will be introduced to my collection of dressage whips." To this, she opened a cupboard and triumphantly showed a series of leather whips of different sizes, neatly lined up. Next to it were collars, belts, metal rings, and padlocks. Seeing that they were holding my gaze, she reassured me, "They are not for you, not if you are good. They serve to cover the bitches. But now I want to see what you have to offer," she said. Her hand resolutely went to my crotch, which she felt firmly.

"Hmm, it looks like you're already a little excited." I blushed again, but before I could speak, Mrs gave me a warningly look I assumed meant she didn't want to hear from me. My cock was indeed swollen by the beautiful face of the strict Mistress who fondly caressed the leather whips and looked at me at the same time, provocatively. Now she clutched my balls and cock with her full hand, which were firmly squeezed my tight underpants. I let out a suppressed moan. Apparently, that excited her. She pulled me to her and whispered in my ear, "Before you serve me, you will first have to show me what I am meant to be so excited about." She ordered me to follow her to a salon and closed the door. She sat down in a luxurious armchair and beckoned to me. When I stood in front of her, she gestured at the carpet on the parquet floor.

"On your knees, your hands on your back." I obeyed meekly and wondered what she would want from me. She stood up and pulled a pair of leather handcuffs from a drawer of a dresser, which she wrapped around my wrists. Then she sat down again and signaled that I should approach. I shuffled over to her. While she looked at me intensely, she unzipped the fly from her pants. A pair of black panties emerged, with a wide slit in the middle, opening to show a smooth-shaven pussy that was already damp and swollen.

"You know what you have to do, don't you?" She asked me. I hesitantly bent down and brought my mouth to her lap. Carefully I started to lick her wet pussy.

"Come on, a little boy, lick my pussy. Don't make me have to ask you twice again," she snarled, grabbing hold of my hair and pushing my head between her legs. I tasted her pussy juices, and my tongue eagerly found a way between her lips. I slurped her cunt juice and now took her whole cunt in my mouth. She let out a loud cry and pushed her crotch forward.

"Yes, come on; lick me then, nice little slave," she moaned. She still pushed my mouth and nose deep between her womanly thighs so that I could barely breathe. My tongue twisted between her inner labia. I gently bit her clitoris. She jerked and moaned, "Oh yes, more of that. Good boy." As I licked her swollen pussy, she grabbed my tie and pulled my head down. Because the tie was already tight, it made me feel a bit dizzy. With her other hand, she again grabbed my balls and started to knead them firmly again. It didn't really hurt; it even felt nice, because my balls were still tightly packed in my briefs and pants. Suddenly she released my tie and balls and roughly pushed me off with the heel of her boot.

"Get up," she ordered. I scrambled to stand up straight, making her laugh, and I couldn't figure out if it was a cruel laugh or not. She loosened my belt and unbuttoned my fly. She pulled my pants down to my ankles and let my cock and balls flop out of their tight confines from the side.

"Come here, you," she said as she watched me follow her instructions. As I shuffled closer, she took my hard shaft between her lips. She licked it for a moment and then looked at me.

"While I handle your boy's cock, you tell me how much you like it, yes?" She questioned. I liked that she made me feel that I had no choice and nodded. She grabbed my balls again and held them in a crook so that I moaned it out.

"Did I hear consent there?" She said threateningly.

"Yes, Mrs," I hurried to moan. She loosened the grip around my balls and clutched the shaft of my penis with her other hand. She puckered her made-up lips and let my cock slide in her mouth. I felt the tip of her tongue working in circular movements.

"Oh, thank you, Mrs," I moaned. My penis now disappeared deeper into her mouth and was expertly sucked. While her one hand kneaded my balls, she ran her fingertips across my bare ass, as if she wanted to feel the contours of my tightly muscled ass. Then she scratched me with her nails mercilessly, which elicited a suppressed cry. Now she also brought her other hand to my other ass cheek, and she planted her nails in the soft flesh. I moaned again. Her mouth slid off my penis and with a sensual tongue movement, she licked the saliva off her lips.

"Now it's time for the big work," she whispered to me in a deep, sensual voice. She let go of me and pulled a leather holster from the drawer and put it around my cock. A leather sliding loop went around the base of my shaft and was tightened so that my penis soon became steel-hard, another sliding loop went around my balls, which was also tightened so that my balls were tight. The ends of both loops passed under me and came together in a metal ring. She loosened my wrist cuffs and ordered me to lie on my back on a low, narrow couch, covered with dark red velvet, while my feet rest on either side of the bench on the floor. I got leather bands with a metal ring on my wrists and ankles. She clicked those rings firmly on the bars of the couch. Then she applied some lubricant to my hard cock, and finally, she stood on top of me. She brought her heeled boot down on my chest, pressing until I gasped, making her laugh once more. She then kneeled over me and positioned my cock at the entrance of her pussy. I bucked my hips involuntarily, wanting to be inside of her as pre-cum dripped from my dick. Leaning forward, I felt her slide down my shaft slightly as she gripped my nipples and twisted them so hard I shut my eyes and cried out, only to have her rock her hips gently on the tip of my shaft making the pain and pleasure confuse my mind. Seeing that I couldn't think straight anymore, she dropped her hips roughly onto my lap, quickly burying my cock into her now soaked cunt and squeezing her pussy muscles, making my cock throb. Then she grabbed my shoulders with both hands using them to steady herself as she pushed her pussy up and down over my penis. I was mounted and ridden by the Mistress for the first time, and just as I wanted to cum, she would slow her pace time and time again. Deciding that she wanted to cum, she jumped up and down faster and faster, and while she was pulling my tie to her, she gasped that I was a horny slave, and she would fuck me hard. Sometimes she let go of my shoulder to strike my thighs with the whip in her hand so that they soon became red. Suddenly she uttered a loud cry and came on top of me, coating my lap with her juices. I felt her cunt juice flow down my stomach and thighs, and her body slackened somewhat. Although I was also quite excited about this, the tight penis holster prevented me from getting what I wanted, keeping me frustrated. As the Mistress rose off my, another explosion of juices covered me, and she came over to me, went down, and again stood on top of me on the couch, but this time over my head. She pushed her soaked pussy against my mouth, pulled my head towards her in both hands, and ordered me to lick her clean. When she was satisfied, she dropped my head on the couch again and kissed me on the cheek.

"Pretty big, little boy," she celebrated.

"Ah, how thirsty I got," she added and pulled on a bell, and Tammy appeared and was ordered to bring Mrs a cocktail.

When Tammy came back a little later with the drink, she asked if there was any service for Mrs and to my surprise, Mrs said that Tammy had to stay a little longer, because 'the boy on the couch' deserves a reward.

"He will take you doggy style. Get in position," Mrs said, stroking Tammy's hair and kissing her on her forehead.

"Come on, bitch, do what you are asked; otherwise, you will be punished," Mrs said, spanking Tammy on her ass and roughly grabbing at her breasts. Meekly the girl sat down on her hands and knees while Mrs released me from the couch and released the penis holster. She smiled at me, somewhat scornfully.

"Now it's your turn to ride her... but first, I have a surprise for you. Also, get on your hands and knees and raise your butt," Mrs commanded. I obeyed her, and a moment later felt how she put ointment on the entrance of my asshole.

"That glides better, you pretty little slave," Mrs said to herself as she massaged my ass with her finger for a moment and then pushed in a large anal plug into me. She pushed it deep into my anus so that it could only be removed with a leather strap attached to the back, making me gasp.

"And now, party time," she said, laughing, letting her dressage whip hit the air.

"Come on, my little bitch, you also raise your ass so that you can be fucked," Mrs ordered. Mrs pushed the girl's skirt up and felt her fingers between her legs to feel if she was already wet.

"Hmm, we have to warm you up a little more, don't we, my pretty slut," she said and took a short whip that she used to whip Tammy's ass suddenly. I could tell that Tammy was fighting to stay quiet as her cheeks turned red from the flogging Mrs was giving her. Breaking, Tammy moaned aloud.

"Bitch, I want to see your pussy juices flow," she snarled at her impatiently, feeling that the girl's pussy was slowly getting wet. She took two nipple clamps from the drawer and put them on her.

"Isn't that better, those clamps on your tits, disobedient slut?" She mocked her.

"And you," she said to me, "give that bitch what she deserves." I stood straight and approached the maid from behind and, without hesitation, shoved my cock into her moist, silky pussy. That's how I started fucking her doggy style. To encourage me, the Mistress tapped my ass with her whip and gave my butt plug a little jerk when she thought my pace was slowing.

"Fuck her you useless slave, please, my little girl. Harder, deeper, and faster, show me what you can do, that bitch must be taken hard, fuck her pussy nice and deep; she likes that," Mrs commanded as she began to play with her own pussy as she watched. Then she changed position and pulled the girl's head back by the hair.

"Your pathetic mouth has nothing to do, wouldn't you lick me, slut?" The Mistress said her sensual voice. The view of the girl getting fucked by me, while I pumped madly trying to cum before Mrs changed her mind made my head spin in excitement. Suddenly I moaned that I would cum.

"Because it's your first time, I will let you, but you won't cum afterward without my permission, do you understand?" Snarled the Mistress.

"Yes, Mrs, of course. I really can't keep it anymore..." I groaned as I felt my climax surge through my cock.

"Then fill her up with your full load," Mrs said, getting up and going to sit in front of Tammy. I could feel myself getting jealous of the way Mrs touched the girl, as she held her head in her hands as she loved her gently. And I felt myself fucking Tammy more aggressively as I came deep inside her cunt. Those words from Mrs drove me over the edge, and my jealousy kept me cumming inside Tammy longer than I had cum before. I squirted a powerful blast of white cream into her soaking wet pussy with an elongated cry.

"Now take it out quickly," she ordered. I pulled back my limp penis out of the girl and swapped positions with the Mistress. Mistress . took the girl by her hair and raised her head roughly.

"Mouth open. I do not want to see a bit of cum left, understood," Mrs instructed Tammy, took my wet penis between her lips, licked off all the juices, and swallowed it.

"Mmmm, that is nice, hey, bitch, just swallow it nicely," Mistress cooed. When the girl was ready, she looked up submissively and questioningly.

"Okay, that's enough for now," said Mrs.

"Go and freshen up and then polish the silver in the red salon. And you," as she turned to me, "you go and freshen up and rest while. I want you ready for tonight," Mrs explained, making my

mind race as to what she had in store for me later
on.

An Unexpected Challenge

What an adventure. I did not expect my wife, Hannah, to tell her friend about our secret. That I had been wearing a chastity cage for a week and had asked her to become my dominatrix. The latter did not come out, because it was not really in her. She couldn't take it all that seriously. Unlike her girlfriend, as I would soon find out.

It was Friday evening, and Alexa arrived by train. The evening started pleasantly with a glass of wine and the typical conversation between girlfriends who had not seen each other for a while.

"Tell me about that exciting thing you hinted at in your last message," Alexa asked at one point.

"Alright. If you really want to know," said my wife.

"I don't know how exciting you think it is,

but Ryan has bought a cock cage," my wife said plainly.

"A cock cage? What is that?" asked Alexa, interested.

"Just literally, a penis cage," my wife explained. It remained silent for a moment, and then my wife looked at me and said, "Maybe you should show her." I had not counted on that.

"Or are you ashamed?" My wife asked with a smile, the kind I didn't know she could make.

"Well, I don't know if I think that's such a good idea," I said, while my temples were pounding with sudden tension. Just like us, Alexa was in her late thirties, but she was still a gorgeous woman whom I had often fantasized about — a bit of flirting, too, but everything had always remained above board. That image would soon change if I followed the situation that my wife created.

"It's not a question," she repeated, "I want you to undress now. That is what you wanted — that I would be your mistress. Well, this is what I want you to do," my wife explained. Where did this suddenly come from? She had not seemed interested all week when I suggested that she should be allowed to become dominant and suddenly this.

"Did he want you to be his mistress?" Alexa asked, raising her eyebrow.

"Yes," said Hannah, "but I didn't know if it was really for me, but look at the worried look on his face. I can tell this is definitely something I want more of. Alexa said, "I thought for a moment you really meant it." Hannah was quiet for a moment, swallowed once, and turned to me. "Yes, I meant that," she said.

"You, go to the bedroom now, and you will be back in five minutes — naked, and then you show your cock cage," she demanded. I realized that this was more exciting than I could have imagined in my imagination. I went up the stairs to the bedroom and started to get undressed. My dick swelled up in the cage but can't go anywhere. On a whim, I reached for the nightstand where I had hidden a buttplug. I covered it with lotion and bent my ass to the mirror. I carefully introduced it. For a moment, I looked at the glittering decorated end that now covered my anus.

"Why are you taking so long," I heard Hannah calling from below. I shot straight, turned around, and took my reflection. Yesterday I had shaved and left only a small, short triangle of pubic hair that pointed to my cage. It didn't look very masculine, but it made me very horny.

Well, and then let it happen, I thought and walked slowly downstairs. I stopped at the door of the room. I took a deep breath and stepped into the room. I stepped inside, and there I stood — nude, with only the transparent penis cage around my dick and a butt plug in my ass. Never thought my wife would ever see me like that, let alone one of her friends. But there she was really sitting on the couch, next to Hannah.

"What do you think?" Hannah asked Alexa, who had undergone a remarkable metamorphosis in the short time I had been in our bedroom. She was only wearing black tights and a black bra. And her thick black glasses, through which she looked at me sternly. I had no idea how this could have happened so quickly, and Hannah read the surprise of my face.

"Yes," she said, "We just sat down and made an appointment. Alexa has always been quite dominant, but her husband couldn't handle it. Not in daily life and never mind in the bedroom. That's why they were divorced. Well, and one and one is two, you will understand. When she just heard of your desire, we decided that she can have you tonight," Hannah explained.

Alexa stood up. She was beautiful but also frightening. There was nothing left of the friendly, relaxed woman I knew. She reached for the coffee table and picked up a magazine from which she slowly began to roll up.

"Come here," she said, with a voice that tolerated no contradiction. I walked over to her and stood right in front of her.

"Well, let me see that case," she said. I

hesitantly took another step forward. She took my balls in her hand and pulled my scrotum forward.

"So that's a penis cage," she told Hannah.

"Good invention. I didn't know they existed. And he came up with the idea that he wanted one?"

"Yes," said Hannah. "And I have to say that I'm starting to get used to it. He has been wearing it for a week now and is apparently beating it. But I have the key, so he stays locked up. I notice that he has a lot more attention to me now. And he licks a lot better too. I even got off the last few times, and that never happened before," Hannah said. I felt my dick swell again when I heard the two talking like that, and apparently, Alexa, who was still holding my case, had felt my excitement too.

"He gets a little excited," she said.

"Let's see if he stays that way." Then she turned her head to me and looked intently at me as she released me, and the magazine started to roll up a little tighter.

"I'll first let you feel what happens if you

don't do exactly what I say. Bend over and present your ass," Elexa ordered. I felt my muscles contract around my buttplug, which the women had not yet seen. For a moment, it was as if time stood still when I realized exactly what situation I was in. Only a month ago, I was just an ordinary man with an ordinary marriage and a dead sex life. We did it once or twice every couple of months. It was always pleasant and intimate, but Hannah never longed for more. And I didn't always insist. Things had settled slowly, and I resigned themselves to the fact that it would stay that way further. If I built up too much sexual tension, I would find my convenience on the internet, and then that would do it. Until the time, I came across that photo of a man with a penis cage - although I didn't know what it was then. A strange sensation took hold of me, and soon, I scoured the internet every night for sites that further fueled my fascination — chastity, usually in combination with female domination. I was drawn to it irresistibly. And gradually, my desire grew not to let it stay with fantasy. And that was successful. Because here I was now. Slowly I bent over for the first time in my life to be hit on my butt by a woman. While I was wearing a penis cage, I had a buttplug in my ass, and my own wife was sitting on the couch watching.

"Turn your ass towards me," Alexa ordered, and without hesitation, I did as I was told. She rolled the magazine in her hand a little tighter and then let it hit my ass unexpectedly. And again. After five hits, she stopped and looked at Hannah on the couch who, to my surprise, began to take off her skirt.

"It makes you as horny as him," said Alexa. Hannah got up, got out of her skirt, and now pulled down her panties. A beautiful sight, bare from below, tightly dressed and cut from above. My dick filled the cock cage to bursts, and I felt come dripping down my leg in careful drops.

"On your knees," Alexa snapped at me. I obeyed and saw Hannah walking towards me and positioning herself in front of my face.

"Lick it, bitch," Alexa said, and immediately, I buried my mouth in Hannah's juicy cunt, as wet and slippery as I had never tasted or seen it.

"I can't wait for Jim to come," she told Alexa.

"He's on his way and should be here soon." Jim? That was Alexa's new friend, but wouldn't he be with him tonight?

"And he's looking forward to it," Alexa told Hannah. It seemed that Hannah was getting wetter than she already was. I was so horny that I didn't care anymore that Hannah would soon be fucked by someone else. As terrible as it would normally have sounded to me, I was so excited by the idea alone.

"Yes," said Hannah, looking down into my eyes. "According to Alexa, Jim has a really big dick, and I want to feel a real guy who fucks me like a whore." At that moment, the doorbell rang, and Alexa said, "Well, there you have it." And then to me, "You open it up quickly," immediately a pet on my penis cage. The women smiled at each other as

I reluctantly walked down the hall to open the front door. Again the bell rang. He was apparently impatient. I had met Jim once before — a solidly built guy with black hair and a friendly appearance. I opened the door and involuntarily held my hand in front of my crotch. Jim looked at me, and a mocking smile curled around his lips.

"You don't have to hide that," he said, "I already know about it." He took his smartphone from his pocket and opened a photo — from me, naked except for my cock cage. "Or did you not know that Alexa had already taken some pictures?" With those words, Jim turned around and entered the living room. He hugged Alexa briefly and then let his eyes glide unabashedly over Hannah's body. He gave her a playful tap on her buttock and pointed to the couch.

"Get ready," he said, while Alexa began to unbutton his shirt. I was a bit lost and felt like I was watching a movie. Or rather, a play in which I myself was also on stage.

"Come here," Alexa snapped at me.

"You just loosen those pants so that Hannah can see that I didn't exaggerate," Alexa said. And so, a new phase of the evening began when I experienced more things for the first time than in all the years of our marriage.

Nervously, I loosened Jim's belt, unbuttoned his pants, and rolled them down his legs. An impressive dick was visible in his briefs. It seemed twice as long and thick as mine. I pulled the underpants down, and his penis jerked all the way up. Should that huge monster go straight into Hannah's cunt? Could she handle that? I looked back and saw how she put her hand between her legs and started fingering herself.

"On your knees and look in front of you," Alexa said and slapped my butt hard with her flat hand. I went down on my knees, and now my face was right in front of Jim's thick shaft.

"Open wide bitch," said Alexa. I had never felt a dick before, let alone in my mouth. But I understood that I should not hesitate and closed my lips around the throbbing veiny rod. Instinctively I put my hand under his balls and began to gently knead them as I gently took his dick deeper into my mouth and started moving my head up and down.

"He has done that before," Jim said, laughing broadly.

"I don't think so," said Hannah, "but he is doing well; it looks like."

"Would you rather do it yourself?" Asked Alexa, but Hannah shook her head.

"This is a beautiful sight," she said.

"It makes me incredibly horny," she added.

"Well, then wait until you see how I can fuck him completely with a strap-on," Alexa said professionally. I heard it, but it hardly dawned on me. My initial uneasiness had given way to pure excitement. Here I was on my knees with my throbbing cock in my mouth, in a tight penis cage while I was sucking the huge cock from the bull that would soon show my wife how a real man fucked. I moaned with horniness, while behind me,

I heard Hannah say it was time for her turn.

"We will start calmly," said Alexa, "first getting you used to it. If you are only used to that cock from him, you will be shocked."

"I am ready for it," said Hannah and lay back on the couch. She spread her legs and pulled her pussy lips apart, giving Jim a clear view of her dripping cave.

"Just sit by it," Alexa told me. Reluctantly I stopped sucking Jim off and got up and approached the couch while I absorbed the image of Hannah. I had never seen her so horny and whorish before, and that was reinforced by her neatly cut hair, well-groomed make-up, and the pearl necklace around her neck — above her shoulders, a neat lady, below that a whore fuck slut. She raised her knees, making her cunt more prominent. There was a chain around her left ankle, and the key of my penis cage dangled from it. I sat down next to her while Jim stood in front of her. She eagerly stretched out her arms and grabbed his dick.

"What a wonderful cock, Jim," she said.

"I can't wait to feel it inside me." Jim did not disappoint her because, without further obligations, he grabbed her ankles, pushed them up, and spread her legs a little further.

"Put it on for a second," he said to me as he huddled the rod a few times on top of her gaping cave by moving his lower body.

"What do you mean exactly?" I asked not understanding his meaning and immediately got a pet from Alexa, who said, "Grab him and lead him inside." And so I suddenly sat there with that huge snake of Jim's in my one hand while I, with the other, pushed my wife's pussy lips a little further apart. He moved his lower body forward, and there I saw that fat cock slowly disappear into my wife's cunt. She sighed as I had never heard her sigh while she moaned in pleasure.

"Yes, deeper, deeper, fuck me. Fuck me hard; I'm your whore, Jim. Fuck me hard." Jim knew what was expected of him and let his dick disappear quickly into her as she moaned all through the night.

Mistress Emily

These friends of mine wanted to teach me a lesson, because, they thought, I have some rather annoying traits. They think that I play a rather dominant role with other people and that I (too often) make sexist comments against women. They also find me rather difficult. Of course, I don't agree with that.

It all started on my 25th birthday. I'm a party boy, and I invited a bunch of friends. It was great fun. I especially had an eye for the women around me and could hardly resist them. After a while, one of my friends stepped forward and asked for silence.

"What now?" I said. It was Charlette, a beautiful girl, whom I always fooled around with.

"Dear Kevin," said Charlette. "You are now a quarter of a century old, and so we think you have earned a special gift. But there is a problem, the gift was too big to take here, and you will have to pick it up yourself. It is a gift from all the girls, and I am sure you will like it." She then approached me and gave me a big kiss. I couldn't help but grab her by the ass and fondled with it until I felt my cock begin to go hard; she just stood there, taking it. We continued with the party, and after a while, Laura came to stand with me. "Just about that gift, Kevin," she said, "You can go get it tomorrow at 5 p.m. You have to go to Hotel no. 68R and ask about Emily there." She gave me a big wink and walked away with her hips rocking. "What a nice thing that is!" I said to myself as she left. In my mind, I had already undressed her, and I saw her beautiful, round bare ass being stuffed with my cock. It got pretty late that night. At about three o'clock, the last friends left, and I took all the ladies in my arms and, of course, took full advantage of their scantly clothed bodies.

The next day I slept in for a long time. At about two o'clock in the afternoon, I got up and took a nice long shower.

"Oh yeah! I have to pick up my present today!" I said, remembering. I quickly dried off and put on a pair of jeans and a T-shirt. The weather was nice outside, and I decided to grab a beer before I would walk to the Hotel. After a fifteen-minute walk, I stood at the door of Hotel 68R. I rang the bell, and through the intercom, I got to hear a woman. It was Emily, and she opened the door for me and told me I could walk on up. It was a beautiful canal house with beautiful high ceilings and a stylish staircase. Her door was already open upstairs. I knocked on the door for a moment, and I heard a call from the room, "Come on in, I'm still busy!" I walked in and stood in a large room that was nicely decorated. There was a large black leather couch and several smaller, black leather chairs. A huge man-sized mirror hung on the wall. I heard Emily rumbling in the room next door. I walked around a bit, and after a while, I heard the door open and turned around. A handsome woman stood in the doorway.

I think she was about 55 years old. What most stood out was her clothing. Although, if you could already call it clothing! She was wearing a black, super-tight, shiny, super-horny suit. I think it was latex and left nothing to the imagination when it came to the shape of her body. From her feet to her shoulders, she was wrapped in black latex. It was so tight it looked like she wasn't wearing anything. She had delicious, full breasts and nice, wide hips. At the bottom of the suit, at her feet, were black pumps with huge high heels. Because of those high heels, she stood in a nice position so that her nice, full ass perky stuck back. It was, all in all, a beautiful, attractive, horny, but oh so dominant looking woman!

"You are early!" Emily said. "You were told that you had to be here at five, and it is only a quarter to five! I don't like measly males who do whatever they want! "She approached me and grabbed me hard by an ear! That's how she dragged me to a corner of the room.

"But I just come to get my present!" I sputtered.

"What?? You cannot get your present! I am your gift!" Said Emily.

"What do you mean, you are my gift?" I said as I got a slap in the face!

"I don't answer to you," Said Emily. "You must address me with Mistress Emily, and nothing else did you understand that!?" I did not know what happened to me and was actually completely overwhelmed. There I stood, like a dick in a corner — helpless against this dominant woman.

"Well, do you understood me!" She screamed.

"Yes, I understand," I said softly.

"Yes, what?" Said Emily.

"Yes, Mistress Emily, I understand," I said.

"Well, that's how I like it. Now, your gift. You have the pleasure of being my slave today. You get a lesson in humility and submissiveness!" I usually have my word ready, but under the influence of this lady, I fell silent for a moment. I didn't get much time to recuperate, because Emily went on again.

"First, I want you to take off your clothes and show me your nice body," she said. I didn't know if I wanted to, but I didn't feel like having my face slapped again, so I slowly started to undress. When I took off my T-shirt, and I could see my bare torso, Emily rubbed her latex glove over my body.

"That looks good," she said. Then I took off my pants and my underpants, and there I stood, naked in front of this stranger. She touched me everywhere as if I was being inspected. The result was that I got a pretty hard cock.

"Well, you are looking forward to it, I see," Emily said, grasping my cock tightly.

"But first, I have something else for you; put it on." She stood in front of me with latex pants. I put it on, and it was terribly tight around my ass. There was a small opening at the front of the pants, and I had to put my thick cock and hard balls through it. It was a very interesting sight.

"You are getting horny of yourself," Emily said.

"I think you're just a horny gay; I see you looking thrilled at your tight cock!" "No horny Mistress, Emily, I'm not gay. I only love women," I said.

"If I say that you are gay, then that's true! You go and stand in front of that big mirror and take a good look at that horny guy in that mirror. I want you to jerk yourself off while you talk dirty to yourself," Emily said. I was put in front of the mirror and had to grab my cock.

"Pull on it! And I want your gaze to remain focused on the horny body of your mirror image! I want you to continue to hold your cock and never let go, and you can only stop yanking when I say so! And now I want you to be horny!"
I started to jerk myself off. I looked at my own body that was pretty well-formed.

"I don't hear you are talking," Emily said, and she gave me a small but nasty whip. She slapped my ass hard and said, "If I don't think you're horny enough, I'll teach you! So horny stallion, you have a nice horny cock. I want to blow your dick. I will milk you empty! I want to see it flow over my fist! You are a dirty slut! You prefer to be fucked, don't you? You are a slave and want to be humiliated! Tell me!" Mistress Emily whispered in my ear as I jerked myself off. I felt that I was about to get ready. I jerked like a madman, and my fist fucked my horny cock. And then it came! Big blobs of sticky cum flew around! I began to slow down, but Emily grabbed my cock and fastened the pace until I was on the tips of my toes gasping.

"This is what I want to see. My helpless little man taking the fucking he is being given like the slut that he is," Mistress Emily said as I was forced to cum again.

"Oooh, yes, spray nice and horny boy. I know you are horny! Let all your excitement escape!" She said as I screamed. She just kept jerking, and meanwhile, the sperm ran in rays against my tight, black latex pants.

"Good slave!" Emily said. "And now I want you to clean your dirty hands! I don't like sticky boys!" Mistress Emily said as she stuck her fingers into my mouth and made me lick them clean. After licking for a while, Emily came to stand in front of me and fell to her knees.

"I'll do the rest," she said, and she started licking my dripping cock. She swallowed my slippery dick in one go. It sounded like Emily really enjoyed my heavy cock, and she sucked my balls completely empty!

"Now it's your turn to lick me, slave!" Emily said. I was forced to my knees, and she put her foot forward.

"I want you to lick my whole body. And you start with my shoes!" She said. The latex pump was held in front of me, and I started to lick it. She turned her foot slightly so that I could take the stiletto heel in my mouth. I started to suck the heel! While I licked her feet, Emily rubbed her hand hard over her cunt, and with her other hand, she grabbed her heavy tits! Slowly I raised my mouth. Along her calves, and then I licked her thighs. I wanted to lick her pussy, but it was still nicely wrapped in the latex package. I continued along the latex buttocks.

"You made me pretty horny slave. I think it's time to release my mature, wet, slippery cunt!" She sat down on a black leather chair and hung her legs wide over the back of the chair.

She fiddled with her hands between her legs, and there the latex package opened! Her soaking wet mature cunt gleamed like an overripe pear, and her labia were swollen with horniness.

"Slave on your knees and show me what you can do with your tongue!" I sat down between the legs of the horny woman and smelled her cunt. I stuck my tongue out and licked her deep in her dripping cave. In no time, my entire face gleamed from the juices. Emily grabbed my head firmly and pulled me deep into her wet crotch. Emily began to moan more and more. In the meantime, she rammed my head between her legs. She ran my whole face through her cunt and sat in her chair, uncontrollably.

"Dirty slut! Lick me ready, whore! Suck with your slave mouth! Lick all my juices!" Mistress Emily moaned. She was panting heavily on the chair and slowly let go of my head, which was almost completely in her hot cunt.

"That was nice slave! You have spoiled my pussy, and it's my turn now!" She walked to the wide leather couch and sat down on her hands and knees. She hung her arms over the backrest, and her wide ass stuck up into the room.

"Grab my ass and lick slave!" She said.

"You should know what your horny Mistress wants! I want to feel that mouth of yours on my ass! I know you have a long tongue, so let it disappear into my ass!" I sat down behind Emily and grabbed her ass with two hands. I pulled her buttocks a little further apart. I stuck out my tongue and pushed it in the ass of my Mistress in one go. With long strokes, I started licking the ass. In the meantime, I slid two fingers into Emily's spacious, still dripping cunt. Fortunately, Emily was so incredibly horny that she allowed it!

"Yes, but I love my ass, boy. Make my ass nice and wet! I want to feel you deeply! Stir with your tongue, Aaah, yes!" She moaned. It didn't take long for Emily to rise to the next high. Screaming, turning, and violently shaking her ass, she came ready for the second time!

She reached back and picked up the whip she had used before. The handle of the whip was a big thick rod with a huge lump at the end! She dipped the rod in a jar of lubricant and placed it against my ass. I was already horny with the idea that the whole device would disappear deep into my ass. When I am jerking off at home, I often put a nice fat dildo in my ass. That makes me so horny. So I'm used to something like this. Emily pressed hard against the bar because she thought it would be tough. But because I have a trained ass, the whole thing fell completely into my ass in one go. It went so fast that even a few fingers of Emily shot with it.

"What do I get?" She said. "Your ass is wide

open! Wait, I'll have something else for you!" She walked to the other room and came back with a huge dildo. It was a flesh-colored giant with thick veins along the pole.

"Let's see what you think of this!" She put the fist-thick jerk against my butt hole and started pushing hard. This time it wasn't all that easy. The circle muscle resisted, but after a while, the dildo won. With a sucking sound, Emily pushed the giant pole in my ass!

"You can't do that!" I cried.

"Of course, I can baby boy," Emily whispered, making my head spin and my cock throb.

"You have a big ass, and then you get used by this fuck rod! Well, let's just sit there and relax! And now I want to be fucked!" Emily said. Again she walked to the couch and sat up with her ass.

"Just slide your pole in! And remember, I want you to fill my whole cunt!" She commanded. It was hard to walk toward her as my ass was filled by her dildo. I stood behind her wide hips and pushed my hard pole into her cunt. Emily's steamy cunt just swallowed my cock!

"And now ram! I love being fucked hard by my slaves!" Mistress, Emily instructed. I banged hard in Emily's mature box, and she also ordered me to put a few fingers in her ass. Sweating, she got up and threw me on the floor. Before I knew it, she flopped down on top of my head, and her leaking pussy flowed empty onto my face.

"Lick it!" She shouted, half hysterically. Wildly licking and gulping, I drained her entire cunt. My mouth flooded completely. I had to swallow a lot; otherwise, I couldn't breathe anymore.

"And what did you think of your gift?" She finally asked as she got off me and walked to a chair.

"It was fantastic!" I said eagerly. Emily was the most commanding woman I had ever met in my life.

It was wonderful to have to be her submissive. She

let me get changed, and as I walked out of the building, I already knew that every time I take my cock in my hands, I would think of Mistress Emily.

Naughty Boys get Whipped!

They often see each other, the gang of four, as they have always been called. Jasmine, Maddie, Jason, and Nick have always been in each other's class from grade 1. The boys are football players, talents at the football club in the city. The girls cannot be beaten in anything related to horses and are successful in dressage. The four are now 18 and have just graduated high school. The boys always look eagerly at the girls in their tight riding breeches and high riding boots, with their whips in hand. They have often spoken about them when they are alone. As have the girls who have never missed a game the boys play in.

The only thing they can't agree on with the four of them is each other's hobbies. Although Nick grew up at the riding school, he has nothing to do with horses anymore, and although they have never missed a game, the girls think football might be the dumbest sport ever. Now on this sunny day, they are chilling in the yard of the riding school, and the boys are annoyed by the chattering of the girls about one of the horses and which bows to put in the mane. The girls enjoy themselves because they know they are bothering the boys. Maddie explains once again that horse riding is elegant, while football is just pointlessly running after a ball. Then Jason suddenly says mockingly.

"You can't call that dressage of yours, horse riding." Jasmine sits down on the edge of her garden chair and looks at the boys thoughtfully.

"You have horse riding, that is the basis. Dressage is the most difficult." The boys are smiling at her. Jasmine looks at Maddie, and the girls immediately have a joint idea.

"Guys," says Maddie, "do you think you could escape from us while we are chasing you on our horses?" The boys look at each other for a moment, a slight doubt on Nick's face, but Jason laughs away any doubt.

"Sure, dude," he laughs, "maybe you are faster with those horses, but we footballers are smart and agile, and if you want a challenge, we are up for it." Nick nods in agreement. Jasmine and Maddie look at each other.

"Ok. The deal," says Jasmine, "you get a 10-minute lead to flee here in the field behind the stables. Then we will come after you on our horses. If you get the forest or the main road, you are safe."

"And if not?" Nick shows some doubt in his voice again.

"Then," Jasmine explains to her brother as she bows to him, "We will imprison you and bring you back to the riding school. We on our horses and you walking behind us. It is for you to hope that there is nobody here." She winks at her girlfriend, and the boys look at each other. They can no longer go back and nod.

"Ok," both boys say at the same time. The girls get up immediately and go inside to put on their riding clothes. The boys are silent and waiting. They know they will have to put in some hard work to beat the girls. Nick even starts a gentle warm-up. Moments later, Jasmine and Maddie come back, and the boys can't help clearing their throats as they see the tight breeches around the girls' nice buttocks and slender legs. Jasmine is wearing khaki color pants, which accentuates her ass and long legs nicely, and Maddie has opted for dark gray. Nick cannot take his eyes off his friends. Both girls have opted for a sleek, white polo, which spans the B-cup of Jasmine beautifully. The tall black boots complete the two pictures.

"OK guys," Jasmine explains, tightening the elastic of her hair, "you can start running. We will wait exactly 10 minutes, and then we come after you."

Immediately the boys run away. They decide to make it as difficult as possible for the girls and split up. Nick, the midfielder with his long legs, runs athletically along the footpath and then into the open field, straight ahead. Fortunately, he is in excellent condition, and within ten minutes, he is more than 2.5 kilometers away from the riding school. As a stopper, Jason is a lesser runner and opts for a more challenging terrain for the horses in the hope that they will not follow him that quickly. It also means that he himself is less fast and less far from the riding school.

In the meantime, the girls prepare themselves and the horses quietly, and after exactly 10 minutes, they rise and urge the two mares with their boots. The first piece they trot next to each other to stand by the open field to look. Jasmine points to a dot in the distance and then looks to the right with Maddie to see if they see the other boy. Then Maddie sees how a branch lies broken on the ground and the fresh impression of a sneaker next to it.

"If you go and get Nick, I'll go and look for Jason," Jasmine suggests. Maddie nods and taps her mare's belly. She is gone, on her way through the open field, hunting for the boy she sees running in the distance. Jasmine goes through the rougher area, which is more difficult, but where her favorite horse gets used to quickly. The rope hanging from her saddle is flapping on the horse's back. To her satisfaction, Maddie notices that she quickly catches up with the boy in front of her. Meanwhile, Nick looks worried and sees and, above all hears, the horse with the rider galloping closer. His heart is pounding in his throat because he has been running for nearly fifteen minutes at a time and is actually unable to. His ankle is already slightly sprained, which means that his pace is a lot slower than in the beginning. Maddie now recognizes the boy and knows that she is chasing Nick, Nick, the handsome, macho one. She smiles at the thought of how she will soon lead him, making him walk behind her horse.

Jasmine has to look carefully because it takes a long time before she sees another sign of Jason.

She is standing still too often for her liking, but then after a few minutes, she sees a figure moving in the distance. She encourages her horse, and they quickly approach the boy. She sees blonde hair and knows that her prey is Jason.

Yes, she thinks, and she encourages even more. Jason notices that his flight has been lost. The horse is quickly approaching, and he has run out of time to escape. He takes a few more steps and then sharply bends towards the forest in one last attempt to reach safety. Jasmine sees it and also directs her mare towards the boy. They quickly cut him off and just before the forest. Jasmine and the mare block the path of the panting boy. He wants to run away again, but Jasmine is agile with the horse, and thanks to the dressage training, the mare reacts super fast. After four unsuccessful attempts and with a throat on fire, Jason gives up.

He leans forward, leaning his hands on his knees, staring at the ground. Then he notices how something falls over him and immediately how his side pulls his arms. Sitting high on her horse, Jasmine has cast a lasso, and Jason finds that she has trapped him. Jason protests, his voice is hoarse, his hair wet with sweat stuck to his forehead. Jasmine knots the lasso extra tight and ties the end of the rope to the saddle. She stands in front of her prey, the defeated boy, and looks at him triumphantly. As she loosens his pants and forces him to get out, she teasingly asks, "Do you want to take back your tough words?" Jason looks at her empty, is silent, his mouth is too dry to talk.

"Ok," Jasmine says, pulling out his shirt over his head and hanging behind his back, "If you don't say anything, I'll let my horse trot back to the riding school."

Jason bows his head, and then it says soft, "I'm sorry I said horse riding is stupid." Jasmine laughs and also pulls Jason his briefs off his buttocks. She sees how his penis quickly becomes stiff and then walks back to her horse. When she is back on top, she looks back with satisfaction. Successful. She has caught her prey and sets her horse in motion, the tied up muscular teenage boy, stumbling naked behind her. Humiliated, Jason looks at how the horse wipes a hornet away with its tail. He hardly feels his legs anymore but has to keep going — the girl who sits tall and proud of the horse gives him no choice.

Nick looks around desperately. He thought he was smart by choosing the open field to reach the road where the girls could do nothing more to him. But it failed. Again he looks around and sees Maddie on her brown mare. Looking around is not smart, because he does not see the stump in front of him. Nick feels how he stumbles and falls powerless on the grass. He wants to get up quickly but immediately feels a knee in his back, followed by a rope around his head. From the corners of his eyes, he sees the nose of a sniffing horse. Two hands quickly slide the sturdy rope around his shoulders, and when Nick wants to free himself wildly from his attacker, he draws his fate. It gives

Maddie the space she needs to tighten the lasso around his waist with Nick's arms in between. She quickly lays a security knot and gives the boy time to get up. Nick looks down at his friend, and she looks back, laughing, after which she fastens the rope to her saddle.

"You came far, Nickie," Maddie says quasi-nicely, "but unfortunately not far enough. That way, you can see that you can't compete with a girl and her horse." The girls have agreed in advance how they will bring the boys back to the riding school. Nick will soon be naked behind the ass of the horse and can only look at the beautiful girl in the saddle and follow her command. His sore legs protest, but meekly Nick stumbles after the mare and her rider.

It is quiet at the stables. There is no one to see how Maddie first walks into the yard with her horse with a naked boy following her. Afterward, Jasmine drives onto the concrete plate with a broad grin, also with a boy on a leash and naked too. Both girls give each other a high five and release the boys. They both grab a rope, after which Maddie pulls her prey, Nick and Jasmine Jason. The boys don't dare look at each other in shame. They slowly allow their mistresses to take them into the riding school.

On the one hand, it is hard for the boys to deal with how easily the girls in the hunt captured them, but on the other hand, both Nick and Jason are protruding with a full, stiff penis, symbolically pointing at the tight asses of the girls. Maddie takes Nick to an empty box, and Jasmine does the same with Jason in another box. Jasmine lays her prisoner on his back and undresses, enjoying Jason's big, eager eyes on her. She strokes her breasts and then takes off her panties. She carefully sits down on him. Slowly she guides Jason's stiff cock into her wet pussy and starts riding the boy as though he is one of the horses she trains. She smiles at him, and he doesn't know how to enjoy what is happening to him. How long has he been jerking himself off to the images of his friends, and finally, it happens?

Maddie has placed Nick against the wall in the other box. Secretly she has often looked at the big bulge in the pants of her friend. Girls at school have been estimating for a while how long Nick's penis is, and now it is sticking up in front of her, like a salute to his mistress. Maddie kneels, and with her heart beating with excitement, she takes the thick, stiff bar in her hand. She licks her tongue over the thick vein that runs past it and slowly starts jerking off Nick. She knows from her girlfriend that both boys are still virgins, and she is too. Carefully as she was a somewhat nervous girl, she takes Nick's rod in her mouth and nibbles on it. It does not miss the effect on the boy. Tied as he is, something unusual happens to him. The pretty blonde who has been hanging around him for years with games, teasing, has his sex stuffed in her mouth and blows him as if she had never done anything else. He almost certainly knows it's her first time, but it feels very natural. Maddie also senses how close Nick is and when a deep groan comes out of the boy's mouth, she releases the cock just to see how thick jets of seed are flying around her. The boy comes trembling and then hangs loosely in his ropes. Maddie detaches Nick from the wall and lets him fall to the ground in the hay. She has just heard a loud scream from Jasmine from the other box and knows that her girlfriend has fucked Jason. She doesn't dare to do that herself, but she is proud of the blowjob she gave her slave. He is still weak and devastated.

"Come," Maddie says to Nick, who begins to stand up. He gets up and lets the girl lead him to the other box. Jasmine is standing naked next to an equally broken, empty, fucked Jason. Maddie pushes Nick towards Jason and lets him fall over his friend. There they lay, two naked teenage boys, trapped and worn out by the two girls, superimposed, limp and defeated. Jasmine leans her naked body close to the still dressed Maddie, leaning her arm on her shoulder. She kisses her girlfriend on the cheek, and the girls look at each other with satisfaction. Both boys can take a quick look at both tight asses while the girls walk out of the box and leave them in the straw.

The girls left the boys in the straw for an hour, coming back to find them asleep. As the girls get closer, the boys spring out of the straw when the girls walk into the box. Their arms are still tied despite their frantic attempts to release. However, they have noticed that the girls make good firm knots, which is, of course, also necessary with horses. All their toughness seems to have disappeared with the boys, especially now that the girls are again just in front of them — dressed in their tight breeches and sexy polo shirts, looking down at the naked boys. Jasmine takes a straw bale and sits on it while she takes a whip from the wall. She taps her knees with her hands and gestures Jason to lie down over her thighs. When, in her opinion, Jason hesitates for too long, she hits the ground with her whip. The boy bows his redhead and moves towards the girl. He can't believe what's happening to him. He can't believe that he likes it. He knows he will get a spanking from the girl, the girl from his class. He climbs with difficulty over Jasmine's thighs, and immediately, when he lies down, his mistress starts with instructions. She is going to give him 25 spanks on both buttocks, and he has to count. If he makes a mistake, the spanking does not count. The poor boy gets a strong beating from Jasmine and halfway through sobs. He loses count. Jasmine rubs his ass lovingly and strokes his head before asking if he would like to continue. Jason snuggles into her thighs and nods his head year, and Jasmine gives him another five blows on both buttocks this time softer than the others, after which the boy hangs limply over the girl's legs, with bright red buttocks. She drops her whip to the ground, gives Maddie a wink, and takes a belt that she has taken with her. Jason allows the collar to be put on without resistance and she kisses his forehead and cheeks as a reward.

Nick has been able to see everything and obeys faster than his friend. The fact that Maddie overpowered him in the field has already crushed him and that she has then blown him here in the box has made a deep impression on him. It no longer comes to him to resist, and he suffers the blows. His cock is hanging between Maddie's legs, and he secretly enjoys the tightness of his stiff between the nice legs of the girl. At 50 hits, the tears are in the eyes of the faithful Nick, and he floats on the edge of cumshot. Defenseless, Nick falls into the straw and feels how his classmate puts a collar on him. He looks up at Maddie for a moment. A strange feeling creeps into him. It looks like something of gratitude that he may be her slave. He looks at Jason, who also has the same look in his eyes as both boys get on their knees and wait for the next thing the girls wish to do to them.

Sweet Challenge

I didn't get a good grip on her, although I always had my arm around her neck. It gave me some defense against her continuous attacks. She was faster than me, more agile, and she always tried to hold me somewhere. My shirt was already completely stretched, and she had already taken off my shorts. I didn't get a grip on her tight yoga pants, smooth and tight when they were sitting around her muscular legs. We held each other in a grip, I leaning my arm around her neck with another arm on one elbow, she with both arms around my neck. It was a status quo for a moment, but suddenly she let go of something and turned, allowing her to throw her weight at me, and we rolled over — me on my back. She quickly popped on my stomach, bent her breasts on my face and held her arms tightly around my neck. I tried to put my hands down her side, but she made herself small and I couldn't move her upper body. Loosening her arms didn't work either, because she had a much stronger grip around my neck than I could get on both of her arms. I started gasping because I had to breathe through the fabric of her top, between her breasts. To get freer, I started pushing my hips up, but she didn't move aside. On the contrary, she only tightened around my neck, her breasts tighter on my face.

I started to breathe harder and started to feel the panic of the asthma attacks of the past. She also panted, but not so heavily, her breathing was regular, that of a trained sports girl. "Can you still breathe...?" She asked. She heard my support. "You can also give up." I wasn't that far yet. Again I pushed my arms with all the strength I had in her side to push her up, hoping she had to let go, but it was in vain. The only effect was that she took more breathing room from me. I was now seriously in breathlessness, in my opinion, and dared, with my asthma history, to stop lying like that. I humbly tapped her arm.

She slowly let go of her tight grip on my neck and sat up on my diaphragm. She looked at me triumphantly, sweeping a few strands of hair from her face to behind her ears. I tried to detect drops of sweat on her face. She had turned a little red from the exertion, but she wasn't tired and sweaty, far from it.

"How did that feel, so helplessly clamped by the arms of a girl?" She asked mockingly, leaning forward and placing her hands next to my head, arms outstretched. I didn't answer and wanted to turn around to get up; this fight was over. Big deal, she had won.

"No! No! No!" She cried definitely, pushing my left shoulder back onto the mat.

"You're not going anywhere. You stay here because I'm not done with you yet. First, tell me why you tapped out." I sighed and replied that I was short of breath and that I am frightened by my asthma.

"Hmmm..." she said, her hands resting on her thighs, "that's annoying dude." I nodded, grateful for her empathy. I found this woman beautiful, despite her strength and wrestling skills, she remained very feminine and empathetic. She pushed her ass forward, over my chest, and bent over my head, grabbing my arms and pushing the mat.

"Let's test how long you can actually breathe; I think you're just a scared wimp." I shook my head.

"No, really, I can run for a long time, but I don't have a strong breath." She put her knees on my upper arms, and she was now sitting with her pants against my neck, looking me in the eye — laughing, my eyes looking back uneasily.

"Don't worry, honey," she nodded at me, "you know that before I became a fitness instructor, I studied medicine. I know how far I can go before you really run out. But..., "she made her smile very broad," you can beg me to stop.

"What are you going to do then," I asked, a

little worried; I just couldn't imagine she was up to something, but humiliate me.

She let go of my arms, but it didn't give me a sense of freedom because my arms were now trapped under her knees.

"Let's see..." and she placed her left palm-full on my mouth. I instinctively started breathing through my nose faster, but that freedom soon came to an end when she placed her right thumb and index finger on my nose and pinched my nose shut. I looked at her with wide, panicked eyes, but she looked back calmly and decisively. My eyes rolled from left to right, but it didn't bother me. I started pushing my diaphragm, but it didn't help much, while she only held tight and pinched my nose. I tried to roll over both of us by turning from left to right and back, but she kept herself pretty balanced, also because she firmly clamped my head and neck with her legs. I did move a lot, but it did not affect her position. She let go for a moment, and I quickly started to breathe quickly. She took her hands away, and I gasped for air. She put her palm back on my mouth and held her right thumb and index finger in front of me.

"Let's go again," and with that, she closed my nose again. I wanted to do all sorts of things but stayed as still as I could. The breathlessness naturally increased, but I wanted to show her that I could handle her training, that I wasn't a wimp. I focused on the seconds, and I was surprised by how long I could last. She looked at me concentrating and seemed quite impressed; I lasted longer than she had expected. Her eyes looked at me searchingly, looking for panic in my eyes. It was killing for me. Where I hoped that she would let me go, if I could hold on for a long time, her eyes seemed to give another message. Her palm was wet with my breath, but she held tight. I couldn't stay in control anymore and let go of all my panic feelings. I twisted my body wildly, spit mucus under her palm, and begged her with my eyes. I wanted to focus the saddest puppy eyes on her and finally, after my feeling after minutes, but of course much shorter, she let go. I started panting, sniffing, coughing, coughing up mucus; everything had to be done at once.

She stood and looked down at me, her hands in her side. I turned on my side to cough better. I noticed how she stepped over me and squatted beside me, stroking my shoulder and her.

"You could hold on for a long time, dude. I didn't expect that from you after your pathetic story about asthma." I looked at her with watery eyes, confused. She got up again and walked a few steps away, automatically looking at her muscular buttocks and legs. She turned and tightened her hair again with the hairband.

"Okay, you ticked once, and we're not talking about your breathing test. It's 1-0 for me. Are you ready for the next round? Male vs. Female?" I lay on my side, my face turned to her, leaning on my right elbow. There was a power in me that wanted me to get up and teach her a lesson, but a different feeling was much stronger. I didn't stand a chance against her, and I didn't want to run out of breath again.

Slowly I started moving and sat down on my knees. I looked at her, and the more I looked at her, the more discouraged I became. The little willpower in me disappeared, and I started a movement that was the only option left, crawling forward on hands and knees towards her until I was right in front of her and saw her lower legs and feet close to me. Slowly I leaned to the floor, pursed my lips, and gave myself to her, humiliated by slowly placing a kiss on my right foot. A shiver went through me and I think her body too. I belonged to her; I was willing to do everything she wanted from me. And it felt wonderful.

My heart was still pounding violently. I watched as instead of having to wrestle her again, she started to take off her pants, indicating that I could remove them completely. I slowly pulled her pants over her thighs, knees, and finally over her ankles and feet. I looked briefly at her panties and, at something above, at the navel that had been visible all this time. I moved forward again, my stomach against her knees, and grabbed the hem of her sports bra. She rocked a little as I pushed it up and she raised her hands so that I could pull the bra off without difficulty. I looked at her breasts and was stunned by their fantastic shape. The bra already made her breasts look great, but they were sensational. Instinctively, she grabbed her breasts in my hands, folding my hands like a soft cup. I stroked the skin and gently rubbed her nipples with my thumbs. In the meantime, I felt my cock rub against her thigh, growing centimeter by centimeter. I sought eye contact and she looked back sweetly and softly. Her nipples became wonderfully hard and I carefully took them between thumbs and forefingers, gently squeezing. I saw her close her eyes and bit her lower lip.

I let go of her breasts and gently pushed her knees apart, making it easier for me to reach her panties.

I felt how the fabric was damp, and she shivered a little at the touch of my lips. I grabbed her panties by the sides and pulled them down much rougher and faster than with her pants. She moved with it. She was in a hurry; she wanted me, my mouth on her pussy. I felt her hand on my head, and when my tongue felt her pussy, I felt a shiver. She tasted delicious, the moisture around the inside of her pussy sat around my mouth, and I felt encouraged to go into her pussy with my strong, practiced tongue. Finding sensitive spots was always the best thing about women and there were also many differences, also in the way they responded. My instructor was of a quieter type, but her breathing became heavier and she squeezed my hair harder and harder. She clearly enjoyed it and I knew I had found her sensitive spots.

It was a strange sensation as she reached for a rope and tied it around my neck rope, while the woman who had bound me so, was about to get an enormous orgasm thanks to me. She began to talk softly, panting, while she had hardly panted during our struggle.

"Oh... oh... yes... please... please... yes..." I enjoyed her encouragement. It was a sign that she enjoyed it and I enjoyed it again. But did she beg for me now?

"Please... please, please continue." I stopped for a moment and looked up at her face. She had closed her eyes and had some saliva running down her chin. She noticed that I had stopped for a moment and opened her eyes,

"Hey, what are you doing now, don't you dare stop!" I smiled and went on. Her sounds became louder, and I felt that she was very close. I stopped for a moment, and she started again, panting.

"Oooh... please, sweetheart... oh, yes". She spoke desperately now. When she had settled down again, she took my head in her hands and gave me a lovely kiss and ran her fingers through my hair as she fell asleep.

My Horny Ex

I'm Jake, 40 years old. In the past, I have had a relationship with Megan. Together with her, I discovered BDSM. I loved being tied up and used by her. When the relationship was over, we sometimes had sex and told each other all our horny desires. For a few weeks, I feel like playing a fun, sexy game again. I spent long time thinking about what I wanted and in what way, and I thought a lot about the sessions with her. We are now more than five years apart, but more and more I think of the hot sex I had with her. I often have to jerk myself off after I think about her; however, this week, I restrained myself and did not get myself off so that my balls were full of cum, I wanted them to be full and heavy for her to play with. Today I take the chance as I know that she has the day off.

The alarm clock wakes me up at six; I get up and go to the shower. With a razor I shave every hair away, especially around my ass, balls, and cock, I shave extra well. It makes me horny and struggling to keep myself from being jerked off. After shaving and showering, I rub myself with oil. I walk downstairs and unlock the back door. I pick up my phone and send her a message

I still think about you a lot; my back door is open. If you want, we can play. Then I go back to the bedroom and get the things I want. I attach two ropes to the bed legs and lay the blindfold ready. From my bedside table, I grab a butt plug and some Vaseline. I put a large towel on the mattress. I see on my alarm clock that it is now 8 o'clock; I still have a good half-hour if she comes. I make a slider on the side of the rope that is not stuck so that I can release myself. I rub the butt plug with Vaseline and lie down on the towel on the bed. I pull my legs up and push the plug's head into my ass. It slides easily inside. I take the blindfold and put it on. I feel right at home with this thing up my ass. I am becoming more aware of my body and environment. I put my hands back and slide them through the loops of the rope, I pull on the loop, and I'm stuck. At first, my world is no bigger than the bedroom, tied to the bed, blindfolded, naked, and with a butt-plug in. I feel my heartbeat in my throat and hear my breathing getting deeper and deeper. I'm waiting for something to happen.

I feel that the tension increases with every breath. My cock is starting to get hard from this situation. I stop thinking of the sex we have had in the past, and as I feel that my cock is completely hard now. I squeeze my butt muscles and notice that I can pull the butt plug a bit in and out. This way, I fuck myself, and I notice that my cock is also increasingly throbbing. I feel like I've been fucking myself with the butt plug for an hour when I hear a car stop. Now the tension is getting big, and I can feel the butterflies in my ass going on to my cock. My cock starts shaking when I hear footsteps on the garden path. I hear the footsteps go in and I hear the back door slam shut.

Yes, Megan has come, I think, and I feel that I am in an extreme state of excitement. My cock starts to rock and shake more and more when I hear her heels on the stairs. I feel my peak approaching when the room door is opened. I recognize the voice of Megan, who says, "Hi Jake." and at that moment, I can no longer keep it and spray my stomach full of warm sperm with the tension.

"That doesn't help me much," I hear Megan say. She says she's going to release me, but she hasn't finished playing with me. She asks me to promise that I would be a slave her orders this morning. I like to promise that. She takes off my blindfold and takes me naked to the kitchen and puts me on the kitchen chair. She ties me there again with the ropes she took from the bed. She helps me with my chair and back up and says she just has time for a fuck. She grabs my stiff cock and pulls it a few times. With her mouth, she sucks my wet prick, and then she sits down on me. She slides her pussy over my cock and starts to grind on me like crazy. She pushes her breasts into my mouth one by one, and I lick her nipples. She is speeding up and I feel that she is always tightening her cunt muscles. After a few minutes, I feel her pussy tighten completely and she comes ready for the second time. Unfortunately, she keeps me on the edgeMegan gets rid of my cock and loosens my hands. She tells me that she still has about 5 minutes. I pull my cock hard while looking deep into Megan's eyes. I feel wonderfully slutty and submissive and soon feel that I am very horny. I say that I am almost done and at that moment, she pulls my head back and starts to tongue me violently while she squeezes my nipples with her other hand. This is too much for me and with a groan, I cum hard in my hand. Megan says she has to leave and says if I wanted to play again, I should always send a message.

Movie Night

Anyone looking at me would never in a million years think I liked what I like. I'm a good-looking, 35-year-old man who always dresses to impress, and that is what the world sees. However, I have a secret and that is that I love to be dominated by powerful women. In my line of work, I am surrounded by powerful women, and with a high-pressure job, sometimes I need to go out and act out the fantasies I often have about the women I work with. When I go out, I like to frequent the adult movie theater a few blocks from my apartment. This theater caters to particular kinks on particular nights and Friday night is BDSM night. Usually, they have something with a Femdom scene playing, and this is what I go to watch. One such night, I pulled my coat on, grabbed my keys and wallet and headed out.

That evening I was in a very horny mood. I had been given a promotion, and the female executives had warmly congratulated me making me incredibly aroused. With me, the hornier I get, the more submissive I feel myself becoming. I knew that I would enjoy tonight as I paid and went into the darkroom. I let my eyes adjust before I saw on the screen a Mistress who had tied a slave and was busy harassing his nipples by pulling on the nipple clamps placed on them. I smiled to myself as I found a seat and sat down, watching the Mistress on the screen. She wore a red and black leather set with black patent boots. Her hair was long and blonde, and her eyes a piercing blue.

Why can't I ever find and keep a Mistress like that? I complained to myself, feeling sorry for myself for not having much luck with keeping a woman interested. The problem has never been me. Moreover, it has been my job. I find that the few times I have interested a Mistress enough to want to pursue a relationship with me, she has been turned off by the hours of my job. I am detective, which means the hours are long, most of the time very irregular and it is all too easy to get pulled into a case and work on it 24/7 leaving very little time to give anything or anyone else any real attention.

As I watched the movie play, I saw a woman come in and sit in the same row as me, three seats away. I must admit, I felt like a completely different person in the theater and looked at her openly before smiling and looking back to the screen. I recognized her immediately. She was the woman on the screen. The situation and the images on the screen made me horny and I could feel the huge cock in my pants getting harder. I shifted uncomfortably as my dick pushed onto my pants, attracting the attention of the woman sitting next to me. I rubbed it slowly through my pants hoping to stop it getting any harder. This made me even hotter. Driven by my horniness, I slowly unzipped my pants and pulled out my rock hard dick and started to pull on it slowly. After a while, I saw the woman slowly leaning forward to see what I was doing. The tension was now almost too much for me to handle. How would she respond?

I decided to keep pulling on my dick, very slowly, I didn't want to get too turned on and cum too early. The woman raised an eyebrow at me, and I was afraid she would leave, but that didn't happen. To my great joy, she also opened her pants. I didn't want to look too shocked but when I saw her stick her hand down her pants, I gasped and jerked myself harder.

"Watch my film," she suddenly said as she got up from her seat and moved to the seat next to me. She sat down and kept playing with herself before she reached her hand out and pushed my face away from her and back to the screen. I watched the film again and saw that the Mistress let her slave lick between her buttocks.

"Lick me, lick me a clean slave," came her voice from the screen, and I cleared my throat as I struggled to kept myself from exploding. The slave did not respond quickly enough, resulting in a firm slap with the riding crop on his already red buttocks. He moaned in pain and quickly replied by matching his actions to the slaps on his ass.

As I was so close, I was actually hoping that something would happen between myself and the gorgeous woman next to me. As I watched the Mistress on the screen, she had ordered the slave to kneel, hands clasped behind his back. The Mistress pulled the slave's face by his hair to her lap and ordered the slave to lick her.

"Lick me, horny little slave, I want to feel your dirty tongue drink my juices," came her commanding tone. After some time, the Mistress threw her head back and came hard, after which she pushed the slave away from her. The slave immediately thanked the Mistress. I looked carefully next to me again. The woman suddenly got up and left the room, leaving me alone. I was still hopeful that something would happen between us, and as a new movie started, I was surprised to see that she had come back, holding something out to me. I looked at her questioningly and took the piece of paper from her hands. She got back up and left the theater and I watched her go before I read the note.

Come to the coffee shop on the corner so we can talk. I didn't need to be asked twice and quickly put my dick away and got up, going to the restrooms before I left the theater to splash some water on my face before heading out into the night.

"You are getting horny with movies like this, right?" It was the first thing she said to me as I sat down in the booth across from her and looked around the shop almost nervously. It was one thing to be so open and bold in a dark theater, it was certainly another to be talking to the same woman in such a well-lit public space. I nodded yes before accepting the coffee she had bought me before I had even arrived.

"Don't you feel like experiencing something

like that?" I nodded again and said, "Then finish that, then come with me," she leaned forward, and I caught a glimpse of her cleavage and I shot my espresso quickly.

The adrenaline rippled through my body and my heartbeat in my throat when we reached her home after a while. When we arrived in the living room, she immediately fell into her role and snarled at me.

"Do you not know slaves how to behave in the presence of a Mistress? Undress, shut up, and stay on the floor here until I get back." Then she left the room and I heard her go upstairs. Silently I started to get rid of our clothes. I didn't get long to think about what was going to happen, because I could already hear the Mistress coming down the stairs. The door swung open and dressed in tight short black leather skirt, pushup bra, towering black pumps with a golden point and a whip in her hand; she walked straight towards me. Only now, I could clearly see what a beautiful figure the

Mistress had. Her ass sticking slightly backward impressed me. She had, of course, been watching my admiring glances for a long time and came to stand in front of me. I saw that she wasn't wearing panties. Her labia were bare and only her mound was slightly hairy. She looked straight into my eyes. She had black eyeliner around her eyes making her look even stricter. I subdued my gaze subserviently down, where I saw my cock jerked up.

"So," she said, "my new slave thinks that without permission, he can get stiff." With the whip, she slapped viciously under my balls, and my erection quickly shrank.

"A little turned on by your Mistress, hey," she continued.

"This is not how a slave works here. I think I'll have to educate you first. You stoop over," came her instruction. I bent down with my face to the ground.

"Deeper slave," and I heard the whip

whizzing through the air, followed by a burning sensation on my ass.

"Ah," I groaned before I dropped to the ground the way she wanted.

"That's better," she said. You learn fast. "From now on, you are my slave. Do you understand?" She asked. We had covered the importance of safe words and the protocol she expected on the way to her home so that upon arriving, we could be in our scene straight away.

"Yes, mistress," I replied.

"Now we can really start. You are here to please me, and if I do not like it, punishments will follow. Is that clear?" She commanded.

"Yes, Mistress," I replied without missing a beat.

"Slave, you still have a lot to learn, not getting stiff without permission and certainly not jerking off, and not at all moaning like a whore. Only look at your Mistress if she talks to you directly. So there is still much to learn," she explained.

"Yes, mistress," I answered.

"Come and see me, slave," she instructed, and I crawled to her hands and knees. I crawled close to her and looked up.

"Slave, I just told you that you could only look at me if I talk to you directly. You're not paying attention, are you?" She asked, almost affectionately. She walked past me. When she was standing behind me, she bent down and spanked me hard, making me have to bite my bottom lip to stop any noise escaping.

"I will teach you to listen, slave," she said as she lashed out even harder. I felt my ass glow.

"Now, let it be clear that you have to pay attention to this slave; otherwise, other measures will follow." She said, giving me one final spank.

"Yes, mistress." I gasped, happy to be able to make a sound finally.

"Sit back in your seat." I took my place next and quietly breathed a sigh of relief. The Mistress approached me and walked around me inquisitively. She ran her hand over my chest and grabbed my nipple. She pulled it on and then squeezed it with her nails so hard that I thought I would break her rule about moaning, trying hard not to pull away from her. She put nipple clamps on me and pulled on them until I squirmed away from her, making her laugh. She came and stood right next to me and said as she tapped my dick against my dick.

"That's better," she said. As she said that, she went with one hand under her skirt and ran her fingers through her slit and then teased herself in front of me. Now she achieved her goal again; my cock jerked up again.

"Slave," she said quietly, "you are disobedient, cheeky, and horny. You are a horny slut and I always tackle horny sluts in my special way." She jerked off the nipple clamps and left the room. When she came back after some time, she had strapped on a strap on. As she walked in my direction, swinging heavily back and forth. I was still on my knees. She came to stood before me, took the dick in her hands and began to make pulling movements.

"Look what a nice cock I have here for you slut. Open your mouth," she ordered, hardly waiting for my mouth to open before she pushed it past my lips. I opened my mouth and she put the dick in my mouth.

"Blow me hard. Yes, and deeper slut," she said, placing a hand behind my head and she started ramming the dildo up and down with force in my mouth.

"Yes, just let it slide down your throat," she really pushed it down my throat, so I had to gag, and tears ran down my cheeks. This amused her. She pulled the dick out of my mouth and smile. She told me to get up and she led me to the table. She pushed me over the table and I knew what was coming.

"Lie down," she said plainly. She pulled the cock through my recently shaved butt crack and spit on it, after which I felt the artificial cock pressing against my anus.

"Relax, it'll hurt less," she said. After which

she pushed the head of the dick inside with a fierce movement. I moaned in pain, so into my fantasy that I could hardly believe this was finally happening.

"Yes, that's nice," she said. I apparently did not confirm that quickly enough because she grabbed my hair.

"You ok, baby?" She asked kindly as she stroked my sides with both hands.

"Yes, Mistress," I moaned. She started to penetrate me deeper and then increased the pace. She now fucked me hard and mercilessly in my ass. While she was fucking me, she started beating on my ass. I begged for mercy and asked her to stop, please.

"It's alright honey, you're ok," she said, as she pulled out and unstrapped the cock. She took my hand and led me to what looked like a spare bedroom. She lay me down on the bed and disappeared, coming back shortly after with a glass of water and a wet cloth. She gave me the water and placed the cloth on my forehead.

"I must say, you are really cute," she said, making me laugh and close my eyes, enjoying the gentle touch of her hand on my cheek.

"Was that your first time doing a scene like that?" She asked, my eyes popping open and the truth being relaxed in my eyes.

"I thought so," she replied to my facial expression. She held me for a while before letting me have a shower and get dressed again.

"If you want to do this again sometime. I had a lot of fun," she said, passing me my coat as she leaned against the door frame of the front door as I stood on the porch.

"I would really love that," I replied as we exchanged phone numbers before saying goodnight.

9 781922 334404